# ON THE ROAD

## with Mavis and Marge

For Aoibhe

First published 2010 by Walker Books Ltd
87 Vauxhall Walk, London SE11 5HJ

10 9 8 7 6 5 4 3 2 1

2010 Niamh Sharkey

The right of Niamh Sharkey to be identified as
author/illustrator of this work has been asserted
by her in accordance with the Copyright, Designs
and Patents Act 1988

This book has been typeset in
Kingthings Trypewriter

Printed in China

British Library Cataloguing in Publication Data:
a catalogue record for this book is available
from the British Library

ISBN 978-1-4063-2184-5

www.niamhsharkey.com

www.walker.co.uk

# ON THE ROAD

## with Mavis and Marge

### NIAMH
### SHARKEY

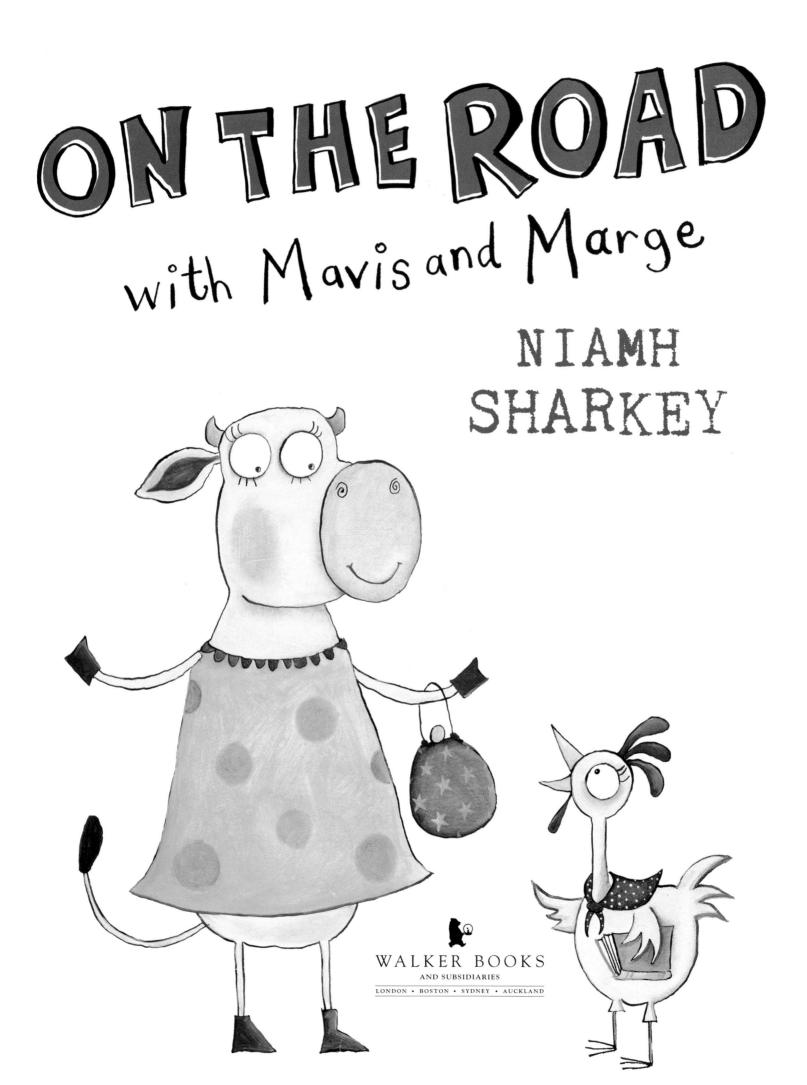

WALKER BOOKS
AND SUBSIDIARIES
LONDON · BOSTON · SYDNEY · AUCKLAND

**Mavis** was different to other cows. She was hungry for adventure.

**Marge** was smarter than your average chicken. She wanted to go where no chicken had gone before.

They knew there was a world out there waiting to be explored.

Ready?

Let's hit the road!

So they took the bike from the barn, said goodbye to their friends and off they went.

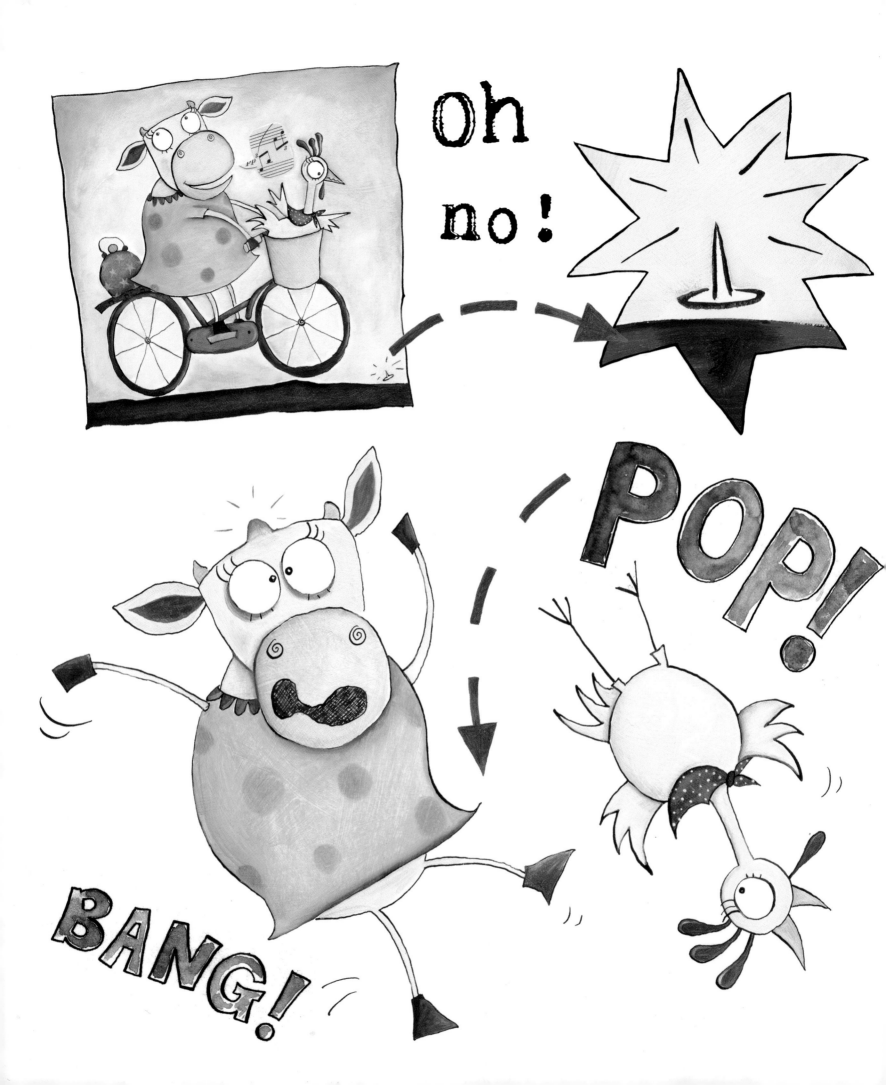

The bike got
a puncture.

So what
luck to meet
Clarence, out
for a spin
in his car.

Uphill ...

downhill ...

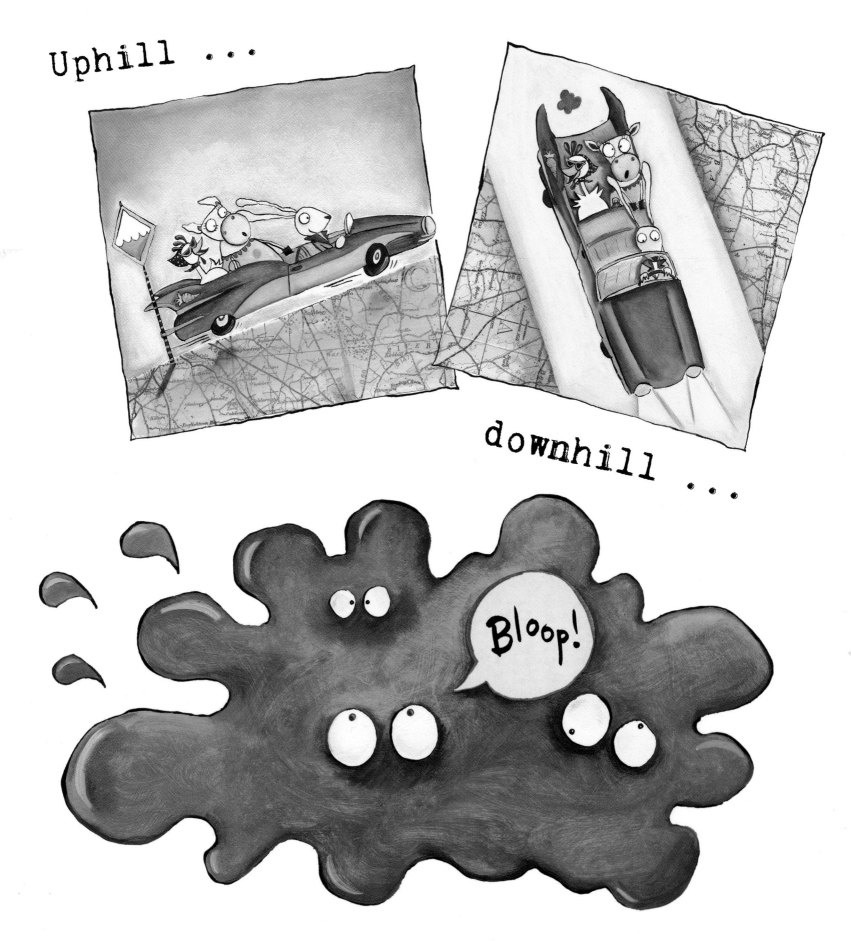

through puddles they drove.

Over bridges ...

through the forest ...

all the way to the ocean.

What luck! They landed
in Benny's boat!

They hit an iceberg!

What luck to bump into Albert.

Mavis and Marge,
Clarence, Benny and
Albert all loved it
on the moon.

But then...

So they
all went
home.

WHEEEEEE!

Life on the road had been a great adventure, but Mavis and Marge agreed...